Dad Goes to School

For Mike Gordon
—M. M.

To my kids, who suffered through
me being home all day!
—M. G.

ALADDIN PAPERBACKS
An imprint of Simon & Schuster Children's Publishing Division
1230 Avenue of the Americas, New York, NY 10020
Text copyright © 2007 by Brenda Bowen
Illustrations copyright © 2007 by Mike Gordon
All rights reserved, including the right of reproduction
in whole or in part in any form.
READY-TO-READ is a registered trademark of Simon & Schuster, Inc.
ALADDIN PAPERBACKS and related logo are registered trademarks of
Simon & Schuster, Inc.
Also available in a paperback edition from Aladdin Paperbacks.
Designed by Sammy Yuen, Jr.
The text of this book was set in Century Schoolbook BT.
Manufactured in the United States of America
First Aladdin Paperbacks edition April 2007
2 4 6 8 10 9 7 5 3
Library of Congress Cataloging-in-Publication Data
McNamara, Margaret.
Dad goes to school / by Margaret McNamara ; illustrated by Mike Gordon.
— 1st Aladdin Paperbacks ed.
p. cm. — (Robin Hill School)
Summary: During Parents Week at Robin Hill School, the students are all impressed
with what one another's parents do for a living, especially Ayanna, who realizes
that the artwork her father does at home makes him very special.
[1. Occupations—Fiction. 2. Parents—Fiction. 3. Artists—Fiction. 4. Schools—Fiction.]
I. Gordon, Mike, ill. II. Title.
PZ7.M232518Dad 2007
[E]—dc22   2006025872
ISBN-13: 978-1-4169-1541-6 (Aladdin pbk.)
ISBN-10: 1-4169-1541-9 (Aladdin pbk.)
ISBN-13: 978-1-4169-1542-3 (lib. bdg.)
ISBN-10: 1-4169-1542-7 (lib. bdg.)

Dad Goes to School

Written by Margaret McNamara
Illustrated by Mike Gordon

Ready-to-Read
Aladdin Paperbacks
New York   London   Toronto   Sydney

It was Parents Week
at Robin Hill School.

On Monday
Katie's mom
came in.

6

"I work at
a knitting store,"
she said.
"Neat!" said Becky.

On Tuesday
Eigen's mom and dad
came in.

"We work at
the animal hospital,"
they said.
"Wow!" said Michael.

On Wednesday
Emma's dad came in.

"I repair clocks," he said.

"Sweet!" said Reza.

That night Ayanna's dad
said, "Tomorrow
I will show your friends
what I do."

"Uh-oh," said Ayanna.
"Uh-oh?" said her dad.
"You are not like
  the other parents,"
  said Ayanna sadly.

"You sit in the living room
and you draw pictures
in your shorts.
Is that a job?"
asked Ayanna.

"We will find out tomorrow,"
said her dad.

On Thursday
Ayanna's dad got up early.

He had coffee.

He got dressed up.

And he went to school
with Ayanna.

"Guess what I do," he said.

Ayanna's dad started to draw.

"You are an artist!"
said Becky.

"Yes," said Ayanna's dad.
"My job is to draw pictures.
What shall I draw for you?"

Ayanna's dad drew pictures
for everyone,
even Mrs. Connor.

"Your dad is super cool!"
said Eigen.
"I would like that job,"
said Katie.

That night
Ayanna's dad said,
"I do not go to an office.
And I do not get
dressed up."

"But you are
the best dad ever,"
said Ayanna.

And she gave him
a big hug.